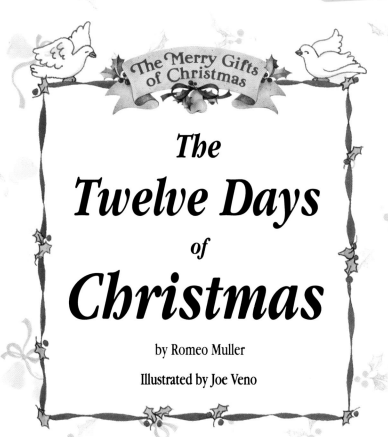

The Merry Gifts of Christmas

The
Twelve Days
of
Christmas

by Romeo Muller

Illustrated by Joe Veno

You know The Twelve Days of Christmas song? It starts, "On the first day of Christmas my true love gave to me . . . ." Well, I know the real story of how the song came to be. I am none other than *the* Mrs. Partridge. It's *my* pear tree the song talks about so much. The story started in the kingdom of the Jingle Merry Teddy Bears and is about three of these cuddly bears.

Princess Merrybell is the most wonderful maiden in the land; she's beautiful, generous, and kind.

Sir Carolboomer is one of our finest knights of the realm. He is a great warrior, accomplished in all the knightly ways.

Last but not least, there's Squire Very Merry. He's clever, resourceful, a little shy, and one of the dearest bears I've ever known.

Christmastime in the land of Jingle Merry Teddies is full of wonder, excitement, and celebration. In fact, these bears celebrate so much that they need to have twelve days to hold it all. Christmas starts on December 25 and goes until January 5. On the last day, they hold the greatest celebration of all, the Twelfth Night Ball.

Every bear knows that anything started during the Christmas season is bound to turn out well, especially a romance. When Sir Carolboomer decided to win the hand of Princess Merrybell, he figured that Christmas would be the perfect time. But then our dashing knight thought some more about his idea, and that's when the trouble started.

"Squire! Squire Very Merry!" shouted Sir Carolboomer. "Go to the castle at once and secretly find out what the Princess wishes for Christmas. If I give her everything she wants, she's sure to like me." The young Squire was not pleased at having to spy on the Princess, but he was loyal to his master and set off for the castle.

Very Merry came upon the Princess as she was making her way to the throne room. He knew that she had just finished writing her Christmas list. But she was also carrying another list—the answers to that week's royal crossword puzzle, which she was bringing to her father, the King.

Very Merry managed to sneak one of the lists away from her, and he hurried off. But he took the wrong list.

The King was left with a list of answers that didn't fit into the royal crossword puzzle, and that stopped him from finishing it. Sir Carolboomer was left with a list of gifts that were quite unusual, but that didn't stop him at all.

"Zounds! What peculiar gifts," he boomed. "We'll have a hard time getting these things, but I'm sure *you* can do it, Very Merry."

The first item on the list was a partridge, and that's where I came in. Very Merry found me sitting in a pear tree. At first, I didn't want to help him. But he seemed like such a nice bear. I agreed, and off we went to the castle.

Very Merry was nervous as the trumpets blared and the page announced us. "A gift for the Princess from Sir Carolboomer."

Princess Merrybell waited on the balcony for us to approach and sang, "On the first day of Christmas my true love gave to me . . . a partridge? In a pear tree?? What kind of gift is that? Take it away."

Very Merry told Sir Carolboomer what the Princess had said. "She's just being coy," the knight replied. "Tomorrow bring her the partridge and the next gift on the list. Two turtle doves."

"Well, you know sir," said Very Merry, "turtle doves are hard to find, especially at this time of year. Maybe another gift would be . . ."

"Find them!" yelled Sir Carolboomer. "Find them and deliver them."

So Very Merry and I found them, and the trumpets blared, and the page announced, and the Princess sang. "On the second day of Christmas my true love gave to me . . . two turtle doves? And a partridge in a pear tree?? This is *not* an improvement. Take them away."

But Sir Carolboomer would not give up. Or rather, he would not let Very Merry give up. We went off to find the third puzzle answer, three French hens. The Princess did not like them either.

And on the fourth day, she liked her gifts even less. "Four calling birds, three French hens, two turtle doves, and a partridge in a pear tree!!! Does your master think I am a bird keeper? Get them out of my sight!"

Very Merry sadly trudged off with his collection of birds. "I wish the Princess was enjoying this more. She is so lovely, and it would be nice to see her smile," he sighed.

The next day called for five golden rings, and Very Merry took great care in presenting them. He arranged them neatly on a fine satin pillow and had a young page deliver them.

He watched quietly from the doorway and saw Merrybell's eyes sparkle as she sang, "Five golden rings!" Merrybell looked up at the young Squire, and I'm sure that for a moment, she was about to smile at him.

But then one of the guards accidentally stepped on a French hen, and the whole room was suddenly filled with squawking, screeching, flying Christmas presents. "Oh no! You brought the BIRDS!!" shouted the Princess. "Out! Out!! Get them OUT!!!"

"**S**he almost smiled, eh?" said Sir Carolboomer. "I'll win her heart yet. Carry on, Very Merry, carry on!"

The sixth day was geese-a-laying and the Princess ordered the guards to escort us out the door.

The seventh day was swans-a-swimming, so Very Merry flooded the palace courtyard to give the swans a place to swim. The Princess might have liked that if she hadn't gotten splashed accidentally. "If you bring one more feather into the palace," she shouted, "you'll end up in the dungeon!"

Fortunately, there were no more birds in the crossword puzzle. The next day we arrived at the castle to hear the Princess sing, "On the eighth day of Christmas my true love gave to me—a COW! A big brown Guernsey cow!"

"Actually, Princess," stammered Very Merry, "it's not so much the cow as it is the maids, the eight maids-a-milking. I thought eight cows marching through the palace might upset you, so I convinced the maids to share this one."

"How thoughtful of you, Squire," said Merrybell. "But I have no need for eight maids-a-milking. Return them and the other gifts to Sir Carolboomer."

On the ninth day of Christmas, Princess Merrybell decided she wanted no more gifts from Sir Carolboomer. She ordered that the royal drummers send this message throughout the land. Whenever such announcements were made, the royal drummers would play the message in code on their drums for all to hear.

On that day, however, the page told Princess Merrybell that the royal drummers had disappeared. They searched the castle high and low but could not find even a single drumstick.

The Princess started to say, "Well, where could they . . ." Just then she was interrupted by a loud RAT-A-TAT-TAT. She rushed out to see the Squire, the birds, the rings, the cow, the maids, and the gift for the ninth day of Christmas. "My true love gave to me NINE DRUMMERS DRUMMING!!"

Once again the Princess was angry and sent us away. But she also wondered to herself how Very Merry had managed to get the drummers to help him. "That is a remarkable young Squire," she thought.

The next day Merrybell decided to stay in bed so that she wouldn't have to see any more of Sir Carolboomer's gifts. When she heard the joyful music coming in through her window, though, she rushed out to her balcony. "What's this? A parade?"

"No, Princess," shouted Very Merry over the music. "It's ten pipers piping." And there they were, playing their pipes as the nine drummers drummed. Even some of us birds joined in and sang the melody.

The Princess looked down at Very Merry as he conducted the musicians, and she smiled a bigger smile than she had ever smiled before.

The Princess actually seemed to be looking forward to our next visit. As we all marched into the courtyard, playing the same little tune, she sang along: "On the eleventh day of Christmas my true love gave to me ELEVEN DAMES-A-DANCING!!" And sure enough that's what we had brought— eleven ladies of the court wearing pink tutus and ballet slippers.

The Dames asked Princess Merrybell to join in and she did. While twirling with the Dames, the Princess somehow ended up in the arms of Squire Very Merry.

The two young bears danced joyfully around the courtyard, and each one of us watching could see that they were falling in love.

That evening, Squire Very Merry and I had a little chat. "You certainly seemed to enjoy dancing with the Princess this afternoon," I said.

"Oh I did, Mrs. Partridge!" cried Very Merry. "But I'm miserable now. The Princess is so wonderful. I think I love her. But I've done nothing but annoy her for the last eleven days with those ridiculous gifts from Sir Carolboomer. I'm sure she never wants to see me again."

I told my young friend not to worry because I was sure the Princess felt differently. And besides, there was only one more gift for us to deliver.

Later that night I left my pear tree and flew off to the castle for a chat with the Princess. "You certainly seemed to enjoy dancing with the Squire this afternoon," I said.

"I did, Mrs. Partridge," whispered the Princess. "I may have lost my temper with him at times, but to do all he has in the last eleven days, Very Merry must be someone very special. Even though those gifts from Sir Carolboomer are annoying, I will miss the young Squire who delivers them once the Christmas season is over. I think I may love that bear."

The next day Squire Very Merry was having an awful time trying to get the last item on the list—twelve Lords-a-leaping. If you've ever tried to get a Lord to leap, you'd understand why.

The task was made even harder because the Lords were feeling especially ill-humored that day from having celebrated too much over the holidays. That gave our clever young friend an idea.

Wearing a disguise, he presented himself to the Lords as Dr. Mistletoe and offered them a cure. "The only way to rid yourself of the 'ill-humors' is to jump up and down until they go away. It works faster if you happen to be in a castle with a princess nearby."

So there we found ourselves in the palace listening to the Princess sing, "On the twelfth day of Christmas my true love gave to me twelve Lords-a-leaping!!!" Merrybell burst into laughter at the sight of the stuffy old Lords hopping and bounding all over the courtyard. Never had she seen such an amusing sight.

That night, the whole kingdom was at the magnificent Twelfth Night Ball when the King made a special announcement. "Princess Merrybell has decided on a husband." Sir Carolboomer stepped forward, sure that it must be him. "She will wed . . . Squire Very Merry."

The crowd cheered and I sang for joy. As Squire Very Merry rushed up beside the Princess, poor Sir Carolboomer fell over in surprise.

Of course, everyone lived happily every after. From that day on, the favorite Christmas carol of all the Jingle Merry Teddies—even Sir Carolboomer—has been The Twelve Days of Christmas.